Puppy Princess

Party Time!

by Patty Furlington

Scholastic Inc.

With special thanks to Thea Bennett

Text copyright © 2018 by Hothouse Fiction
Cover and interior art copyright © 2018 Scholastic Inc.

All rights reserved. Published by Scholastic Inc., *Publishers since 1920*, 557 Broadway, New York, NY 10012, by arrangement with Hothouse Fiction. Series created by Hothouse Fiction. SCHOLASTIC and associated logos are trademarks and/or registered trademarks of Scholastic Inc. PUPPY PRINCESS is a trademark of Hothouse Fiction.

The publisher does not have any control over and does not assume any responsibility for author or third-party websites or their content.

ISBN 978-1-338-13428-5

10 9 8 7 6 5 4 3 2 1   18 19 20 21 22

Printed in the U.S.A. 40
First printing 2018

Book design by Baily Crawford

Table of Contents

Petrovia Royal Family

Rosie

Queen Fifi

King Charles

Rocky & Rollo

Chapter 1

The Very Bubbly Bath

At the top of the tallest tower of Pawstone Palace, a small white puppy named Rosie was in her beautiful, sparkly bedroom. She was supposed to be sitting quietly and combing out her curly tail. But instead she was doing something much more fun—playing a game of tag!

Rosie was the daughter of King Charles

and so, of course, she was a princess. One day Princess Rosie would be queen and rule over the whole of Petrovia. Right now, however, she was having so much fun romping with her two little brothers, Rocky and Rollo, that she'd forgotten all about being a princess.

"Woof! You'll never catch me!" Rosie barked, running so fast that she skidded right across the shiny marble floor.

"Yes, we will!" Prince Rocky yelped, chasing after his sister. He was round and cuddly, like her, and they both had soft, curly fur. But Rocky's ears were longer and floppier.

"We'll get you, Rosie!" Prince Rollo

growled, trying to look fierce. This was quite easy for him, because he had a big black spot over one eye that made him look like a pirate. But once you spent time with him, you could see that his brown eyes were actually very friendly, even when he was growling.

"Help!" squeaked Rosie, leaping up onto her bed and pretending to be scared.

Rosie's bed had a pink satin bedspread decorated with the royal paw-print symbol and lots of velvet cushions. It was very big . . . and very bouncy!

"Look out, Rosie!" Rocky and Rollo scrambled up after her.

Swoosh! Their paws dragged the bedspread off the bed, straight down onto the floor.

"Oh no!" Rollo whined. "Mom will be angry!"

Queen Fifi didn't approve of puppies bouncing on beds, and she certainly didn't approve of bedspreads on the floor.

(Queen Fifi didn't approve of being called "Mom" either. She preferred "Your Majesty.")

"Don't worry about it," Rosie yapped. "We'll put it back later!"

She jumped off the bed and landed on a fluffy rug.

Rocky and Rollo came chasing after her. Rosie giggled and suddenly had a fantastic idea. Her brothers could never resist a game of catch!

Rosie tugged the glittering diamond tiara from her head and threw it across the room like a sparkly Frisbee.

"Fetch!" she barked.

Rocky and Rollo leaped to catch the tiara, and at that very moment, the door to Rosie's bedroom creaked open.

"Princess Rosie?" said a prim voice.

Rocky and Rollo crashed into each other in midair, and the tiara hit the floor with a clatter!

"Ouch!" Rocky squealed as he and his brother landed in a heap on the ground.

"Goodness gracious! What's going on in here?" A gray rabbit wearing a white nurse's cap hopped into the room. Her name was Priscilla, and she was Rosie's lady-in-waiting.

It was Priscilla's job to comb Rosie's fur and make sure she had a bath. It was Priscilla who washed and ironed the silk ribbons that Rosie wore in her fur. And it was Priscilla who polished Rosie's tiara so it shone as bright as the stars in the sky.

Most important of all, Priscilla made sure that Rosie behaved like a proper puppy princess. Priscilla had beady black eyes that didn't miss a thing, and her long ears could hear the tiniest sound. Noisy, rough games were definitely not allowed!

Whenever Rosie did something that Priscilla didn't approve of, her lady-in-waiting would twitch her nose and say "Huff!" If Rosie did something REALLY bad, Priscilla would roll her eyes and say, "Huff, huff, huffity-huff!"

"Get up at once, you two! That is no way for royal puppies to behave!" Priscilla said to Rocky and Rollo. "Your mother, Her Highness, must get ready for the Royal Garden Party. Princess Rosie, where are you? It's bathtime!"

Rosie's brothers scampered away to play somewhere else, and Rosie dived under her bed to hide. Priscilla was always showing up and ruining everything just when a game was getting really exciting. Bathtime? No way!

Unfortunately, Rosie was hiding under

the farthest corner of the bed, where Priscilla's feather duster had never been able to reach. It was very dusty there, and Rosie's nose was itching.

"Ah! AH! CHOOO!" she sneezed.

"Oh, there you are, Princess!" Priscilla hopped over. "Out you come!"

But Rosie was too quick for her lady-in-waiting. She wriggled out from under the bed, dodged past Priscilla, and raced out onto the landing outside her bedroom.

"Oooof!" Rosie gasped as she ran straight into a huge golden Maltese wearing a large crown studded with rubies and emeralds.

King Charles was sneaking up to his

study for his afternoon nap, carrying a silver platter of dog biscuits.

"What, what, what?" he spluttered.

"It's only me, Dad," Rosie explained. "I'm running away because I don't want to have a bath. I want to keep playing."

"Rosie! Come back here!" Priscilla called from the bedroom.

"Now, now, Rosie," the king said, patting her on the head with one of his big velvety paws, "I'm sure your lady-in-waiting knows best. Here, have a treat, that'll cheer you up. These are really delicious."

He held out the platter, but before Rosie could help herself to one of the palace cook's tasty biscuits, there was a click of nails on the

marble floor. A very elegant white Maltese, also wearing a crown, came trotting up and whisked the platter away from King Charles.

"Your Highness," Queen Fifi said, blinking her long, curly eyelashes reproachfully. "The party is happening soon, Charles! You'll ruin your appetite for dinner."

Then she looked at Rosie and wrinkled

her brow. "Where's your tiara, my dear? And why are you looking so messy? The guests will be arriving soon and you must be ready to greet them."

Priscilla hopped over to join them. "I'm sorry, Ma'am! The bath is run, everything's ready, but I couldn't find the princess."

"Hmmm! Really?" Queen Fifi said, giving Rosie a pointed look. Rosie knew what that look meant. There was no use arguing with the queen. Tail between her legs, Rosie slunk off to have her bath . . .

"Why do I need to take a bath?" Rosie grumbled as Priscilla led her to the bathroom. "I just had one three days ago!"

"A princess must ALWAYS be clean. She must NEVER look messy." Priscilla pointed to the bathtub, which was made from snow-white marble, with gleaming golden taps.

"Oh, poo!" Rosie said.

"Huff!" Priscilla's nose twitched. "A princess is ALWAYS polite. She must NEVER be rude. In you go!"

"Oh, all right then. Whee!" Rosie jumped up and dived in with a splash.

Whoosh! Rosie's tail knocked over a big bottle of bubble bath on the edge of the bathtub.

"Huff, huff! A princess must ALWAYS

move slowly and gracefully! She must NEVER jump around!"

Rosie wasn't listening. There was a lovely smell of lavender as bubble bath poured out of the bottle into the bath. *Mmm! Lovely!* Rosie thought.

"A princess ALWAYS uses just a little bit! She must NEVER be wasteful!"

Rosie swished her paws in the water to make a mountain of bubbles.

Priscilla's eyes rolled and her nose was twitching so much that she could only say, "Huff, huff, huffity-HUFF!"

But Rosie knew exactly what Priscilla meant.

"But I love lots of bubbles!" she said. "And I didn't mean to knock the whole bottle over."

"A princess must ALWAYS be careful." Priscilla batted a big bubble away in annoyance. She picked up a washcloth and began to scrub hard behind Rosie's ears.

There was no point in arguing. Priscilla didn't like laughing or bubbles or jumping—in fact, she didn't seem to like fun at all!

There are so many wonderful things here in the palace, and I'm not supposed to enjoy any of them, Rosie thought.

There were toys to chew, balls to chase, and delicious foods to eat. There were gardens to run around in, marble banisters to slide down, and bouncy beds to jump on.

If only I had a friend, Rosie thought. *Then I wouldn't have to spend every day with Priscilla, the most boring and huffy animal in the world. If I had a friend, we could play all day. We could even explore outside the palace!*

A shiver of excitement ran through the little puppy as she imagined how fantastic it would be to run through the forest of Petrovia, and meet all the animals who lived in the villages there.

"You're clean now, Rosie," Priscilla said. "Out of the tub!"

At last! Rosie climbed out of the bath. Then she gave herself a good shake, making bubbles and water fly all over the bathroom.

"Bye, Priscilla! Thanks for the bath!" Rosie barked. "See? I remembered to be polite!" she added as she headed for the door.

Priscilla grabbed Rosie by the tail. "Stop! We're not done yet, Princess."

"Nooo!" Rosie groaned as Priscilla rubbed her fur dry with a fluffy towel.

"A princess must ALWAYS have shiny, silky curls . . ." Priscilla said.

"Ouch!" Rosie cried as Priscilla untangled her curly fur with a silver comb.

"And lots of pretty ribbons!" Priscilla tied pink bows tightly onto Rosie's curls.

"Ugh!" Rosie grumbled. She hated wearing silly bows.

Then Priscilla picked up a bottle of perfume and sprayed it all over Rosie. "A princess must always smell fresh and pretty!" she said.

"Yuck!" Rosie coughed. "I'd much rather smell like grass from the garden than stinky Pretty Pooch perfume! Am I done yet, Priscilla?"

"One last thing," said Priscilla. She placed Rosie's sparkling tiara on top of her head. "There. Now you are a perfect puppy princess!"

"Yay!" Rosie barked, and she raced out of the bathroom.

But she didn't get far. Her pink bows flopped over her eyes so she couldn't see where she was going. She collided with something hard and round.

CRASH!

Chapter 2

A Daring Plan

"Ooops!" Rosie yelped. "What was that?"

"It was ME!" croaked a furious voice from the floor.

Rosie looked down and saw a very old and very angry tortoise spinning on his back, his wrinkly legs waving in the air.

"Oh no!" Rosie whimpered. "Sorry, Theodore!"

"Aah!!" The tortoise groaned, waving his scaly feet in the air. "I can't get up!"

Theodore was King Charles's butler, and one of the most important people in the palace. He looked very funny lying upside down on his shell, but Rosie knew she shouldn't laugh.

"I'm sorry," said Rosie. "I didn't mean to knock you over!"

"You should look where you're going, Your Highness!" Theodore sounded very grumpy.

Rosie pushed Theodore with her paws to flip him the right way up, but his shell was too heavy. She couldn't budge him at all.

"Try a little harder," he grumbled. "I'm

supposed to be preparing for the garden party."

A sharp bark echoed down the corridor. It was Queen Fifi.

"Theodore, what are you doing?" she yipped. "We have so much to do!"

"Sorry, Ma'am," Theodore said. "The princess and I just had a little—er—collision."

"Rosie?" Queen Fifi growled. "Did you knock our butler over *again*?"

"I didn't see him," Rosie explained. "My ribbons got in the way."

Just then, her father came out of his study, stretching his hind legs and yawning.

"Hello, hello!" King Charles looked down at Theodore. "Taken a fall? Let's get you right side up! Come on, Rosie, lend us a paw!"

With her dad's help, it was easy to tip the old tortoise back onto his feet again.

"Thank you, Your Majesty," Theodore mumbled as he crept slowly toward the stairs.

King Charles wagged his feathery tail. "No harm done."

"Hmmm." Queen Fifi didn't look very pleased. "It's lucky that Theodore has such a thick shell. You really must be more careful, Rosie. Try not to trip over the guests at our party!"

"Of course not!" Rosie promised, and then she had a fantastic idea. "Before the party starts, may I play in the garden for a while?"

"Good thinking!" King Charles woofed cheerfully. "Get out in the fresh air! Run around and let off some steam!"

Queen Fifi frowned.

"*Please*," Rosie begged. "I promise to stay clean for the party."

"I suppose so—just for a little while." Queen Fifi looked very serious. "But Priscilla needs to go with you. And you must absolutely stay out of trouble. Our guests will be very disappointed if you are late."

Rosie didn't hear the last of what the queen said, because she was already scampering downstairs, her tail wagging and her ribbons fluttering like pink butterflies!

"Yippee!" Rosie squealed as she bounded over the palace lawn. The grass felt lovely and cool under her paws. She sniffed the air joyfully, breathing in the sweet smell of flowers and the earthy scent of the soil.

Rosie looked around for her lady-in-waiting. Priscilla was a long way behind her, hopping past the big tent where the garden party was going to be held. Hundreds of flags flapped from the palace towers to welcome the guests. Each flag had a big red paw print in the middle, to show it was the kingdom of Petrovia's official flag.

Rosie ran until she was at the edge of the garden, where a grassy slope stretched down to a tall stone wall.

"Come on," Rosie barked. "Let's roll down the hill"

"No, no, no," Priscilla panted, trying to catch up. "We might get our fur dirty."

Rosie didn't hear her. "Wheeee!" she shouted as she rolled all the way down the slope to a mossy little hollow beside the wall.

"Come back up here!" Priscilla shouted.

Rosie scampered back to the top and shook all the bits of moss out of her coat.

"Okay, okay. Let's play hide-and-seek in the bushes, instead."

"Huff! I don't think so." Priscilla's nose

twitched as she fussed over Rosie's pink bows. "We'll get leaves stuck in our fur. What we'll do is go for a nice, calm walk along the path."

Oh, this is sooooo *boring*, Rosie thought as she dawdled along behind her lady-in-waiting.

On the other side of the garden wall, she could see tall trees, green hills, and a little village in the distance. The chimneys sent puffs of white smoke into the air. Rosie thought they looked very cute.

"Can we go there one day?" Rosie asked.

"What for?" Priscilla sniffed. "You are the luckiest puppy alive to live in such a beautiful palace, with such a wonderful garden. Why would you ever want to go outside the palace walls?"

"Have you been there, Priscilla? What's it like?"

"It isn't polite to ask so many questions," the rabbit replied.

"Yoo hoo! Rosie!"

Rocky and Rollo were playing tug-of-war with a big bone.

Rosie raced over to them. "I bumped into Theodore again," she told her brothers. "He looked so funny."

She rolled onto her back and waved her paws in the air, just like the old tortoise had done.

"Hee, hee, hee!" Rocky and Rollo laughed so hard they dropped their bone.

"Rosie!" Priscilla said, hopping over. "That is most unladylike behavior!"

"Oops," Rollo whispered. "Quick, we'd better bury our bone before Priscilla tries to take it from us!"

The two princes scampered over to a flower bed and started digging a hole.

"Stop making a mess, you naughty pups!" Priscilla huffed. She hopped over to the flower bed just as Rocky kicked up a big clump of earth.

Whoosh! It flew through the air.

Whump! It hit Priscilla right on the nose!

Priscilla's white cap was covered in mud. There was soil on her whiskers and on her pink nose. Rosie had to look away to stop herself from giggling.

"Huffity, huffity!" the bunny cried angrily, rubbing her dirty face with her paws. "You three are like a pack of wild dogs! I'm going to tell the king and queen what you did." Priscilla stormed off, shaking dirt out of her long ears.

Rosie lay down on the warm grass as her brothers started digging again. The sun felt lovely on her fur, and she watched a pretty orange butterfly flit from flower to flower.

"What are you up to, you scamps?" A

squirrel with a tweed cap and a bushy tail was pushing his wheelbarrow over the lawn. It was Hamish, the palace gardener. "Don't you spoil my flowers. Her Majesty needs them looking good for the party."

"We're not hurting the flowers," Rocky explained. "We're just hiding our bone."

"Oh yes, I see!" Hamish said with a grin. "Better help you out, then."

He got a big spade out of the wheelbarrow and shoveled earth into the hole until it was full again. Now nobody could tell there was a bone hidden there.

"Thank you!" Rocky and Rollo barked together. They ran away over the lawn to play a game of tag.

"Young rascals!" Hamish chuckled. "They're just like their father."

"What do you mean?" Rosie asked curiously.

Hamish sat down on the grass beside her. "Not many people know this, but when he was just a wee pup, His Majesty dug a hole under the garden wall. When he came up from his digging, he found himself on the other side! He had tunneled right out of the garden!"

"Really?" Rosie was surprised. These days her father preferred taking long naps to digging long tunnels!

"Oh yes! What an adventure that was! Well, I must get going."

Hamish trundled his wheelbarrow away and started cutting roses for Queen Fifi.

Then Rosie heard Priscilla's voice, calling from the other side of the garden. "Princess Rosie? The party is starting soon. Where are you? I must make you clean and tidy again!"

Rosie groaned. *Oh no*, she thought in dismay. *She'll make me take another bath!*

She looked around wildly for somewhere to hide. And then she had an idea. It was one of the best ideas she'd ever had. It was so good it made Rosie's tail wag.

She knew she needed to be fast, before Priscilla spotted her. Quick as a flash, she ran back to the slope and rolled down to the mossy hollow by the wall. She took off her tiara and hid it under a leaf, so it wouldn't get dirty. Then, she began to dig.

"If Dad did it, so can I," Rosie said to herself, pushing soil out of the way with her paws.

Soon, the hole was bigger than Rosie. She dug and dug, tunneling deep under the wall. The cold, damp earth pressed against her. Ahead of her she could only see darkness.

"Keep going, Rosie," she told herself. "It can't be much farther now . . ."

Rosie pawed at the soil, sending clumps of dirt flying behind her. Suddenly, a tiny beam of light peeked through the gloom. Rosie pushed through the soil until, at last, she popped her head out.

Blinking in the bright sunlight, she gazed around in wonder. "Priscilla will never find me here," she whispered to herself.

She'd done it! Rosie was on the other side of the palace wall!

Chapter 3

New Friend

Rosie scrambled out of the hole. All around her, pine trees stretched up into the sky. Birds chirped and twittered merrily from their branches. Under her paws, the moss felt soft and springy, and pretty little white flowers grew everywhere.

The puppy princess stood up and shook the dirt out of her curly ears.

That's better, she thought, tugging off the

only pink ribbon that hadn't fallen off while she was digging.

Rosie couldn't wait to explore!

"I'd better follow the path," she told herself. "I don't want to get lost."

As she headed into the forest, she heard a sound coming from high in the treetops.

That's a funny-sounding bird, Rosie thought.

"Meee-ow!" There it was again, a little louder.

Rosie stared up into the branches. They were covered in thick green pine needles.

"Hello?" Rosie called, her heart beating fast. "Who's there?"

"Meeee!" cried a little voice.

Two bright blue eyes looked down at

Rosie. They belonged to a small, fluffy, gray creature.

"You're not a bird," Rosie said. "You're a kitten!"

"Please, can you help me?" the kitten meowed. "I'm stuck."

"Can't you climb down?"

"I tried, but I'm too scared. I've never been this high up before."

"Hang in there!" Rosie said. "I'll see what I can do."

She scurried around the tree trunk, looking for a way to climb up. All the branches were too high for her to reach.

Rosie stood on her hind legs and tried to pull herself up the tree with her front paws. But her claws were too short and she couldn't get a grip. Puppies are good at digging, but not so good at climbing!

"Help!" meowed the kitten.

"Don't panic!" Rosie said. "I just need to have one of my ideas."

She lay down and put her paws over her eyes to help her think better. The mossy ground felt very soft underneath her. It didn't take long for Rosie to come up with a very smart idea. *Swish! Swoosh!* Her tail wagged with excitement.

Rosie quickly scooped up a big pile of moss and placed it at the bottom of the tree.

"There you go," she told the kitten. "Now you can jump down and land safely on here."

"But it's such a long way down!" the kitten cried.

Rosie bounced up and down on the pile of moss to show the kitten how soft and springy it was.

"You'll be fine!" she called. "Climb down as far as you can and then jump!"

The kitten slowly crawled down from branch to branch. She was trembling so much that all the pine needles were shaking. When she got to the bottom branch, she froze.

"Don't worry," Rosie reassured her. "I'm right here for you."

"*Meeeeeee-ow!*" the kitten yowled as she

let go. She tumbled down, twisting in the air, and landed on her feet. *Boooiiing!*

The kitten looked very relieved. "Phew! That didn't hurt at all! The moss is really soft. Thank you so much! I thought I was going to be stuck up in the tree forever. My name's Cleo, by the way. Who are you?"

"I'm—er . . ." Rosie looked down at her muddy paws. There were pine needles all over her fur, and a bit of moss on the end of her nose, too. Nobody would ever believe she was a princess. "My name's Rosie," she said.

"Wow!" Cleo said. "That's the same name as the princess who lives in the palace!"

"Yes, I guess it is," Rosie said. "What

were you doing up in the tree, Cleo?" she asked, changing the subject.

"I'm not old enough to go to the Royal Garden Party, so I climbed the tallest pine tree I could find because I wanted to see the palace," the kitten explained. "It's so beautiful, with its tall towers and all its flags flying. I wish I could live there like Princess Rosie. She's so lucky!"

Rosie looked down at her paws again. "Maybe. But I bet it's lonely sometimes, being a princess . . ." She hoped Cleo didn't notice how embarrassed she was, but the kitten was scampering around picking little flowers.

"It's my turn to have an idea," she said.

"I hope you like it, Rosie!" Cleo came over and dropped the flowers on the ground. "Let's make daisy chain crowns," she purred. "Then we can pretend to be princesses!"

Rosie shook her head so hard her curls fell into her eyes. She didn't want to go back to being a princess yet, not even a pretend one. "No. I don't want to be a princess," Rosie said. "But I'd love to make a daisy chain. Will you show me how?"

"Of course!" Cleo meowed.

They sat down side by side in the sunshine, cushioned by the soft moss.

"See, you make a little hole in the stem of one daisy, and then you thread the stem of the next one through. Got it?" Cleo asked.

Rosie nodded her head. They worked until each of them had a long chain made from white, pink, and yellow daisies.

Cleo twisted her chain to make a circle, and then she put it over Rosie's head.

"Ta da! Now you've got a necklace."

"Thanks, Cleo!" Rosie said. The soft daisy chain felt much nicer than any of the heavy jeweled collars she had back at the palace.

She popped her own daisy chain over the kitten's head. "Now you've got one, too!"

"We match!" Cleo purred. "Let's make bracelets for all our paws, too!"

Soon, Rosie and Cleo were wearing so many daisies they nearly blended in with the flowery forest floor!

"What do you want to play next, Rosie?" asked Cleo.

Rosie sat very still for a moment as she thought. The wind whistled through the pine trees and ruffled her fur. Rays of sunshine shone down through the tree branches, making a pretty pattern on the forest floor.

Who else lives here, in this beautiful place? Rosie wondered. She really wanted to find out. Would Cleo go with her? Or would she be like Priscilla, and want to stay sitting quietly on a moss cushion?

Rosie took a deep breath.

"Let's pretend we're explorers and see what we can find in the forest. Maybe we'll make some other new friends."

"Mee-ow!" Cleo clapped her paws. "That's a great idea!"

Rosie let out a yelp of delight and sprang to her feet. At last, she was going to have an adventure! And best of all, a new friend was going to share it with her!

As Rosie ran off through the trees with Cleo, her tail wagged faster than it ever had before!

Chapter 4

Friends to the Rescue!

Rosie and Cleo scampered along the forest path together.

"Hey, Cleo! See that big oak tree ahead?" Rosie yapped. "I'll race you there!"

"Give me a head start, then!" the kitten meowed. "Your legs are longer than mine."

"Okay! I bet I'll still win, though!"

"This is fun!" Cleo bounded away, her tail sticking up like a fluffy question mark.

She ran so fast she was nearly at the big tree before Rosie caught up.

Rosie had just overtaken Cleo when she saw something strange hanging from a tree. She skidded to a halt. *Ooomph!* Cleo ran straight into Rosie's bottom.

"*Meee-OW!*" Cleo said.

"Gosh, sorry!" Rosie barked. "Are you okay?"

"I'm fine." Cleo rubbed her face with her paw. She giggled. "Just give me some warning next time you're going to stop suddenly like that!"

What Rosie had seen was a big piece of bark tied to a branch. It had some words written on it.

"Oak Tree Hollow..." Rosie read. "What's that?"

"It must be the name of this village," Cleo explained.

"What village? There aren't any houses. All I can see are those big acorns over there."

Rosie was about to say they were the biggest acorns she'd ever seen, when a door opened up in one of them and a little gray squirrel with tufty ears jumped out.

The big acorns *were* the houses! Each one had its own tiny door, a round window, and a thick, mossy roof to keep the rain out.

"Hello!" Rosie barked, but the squirrel

bounded away and disappeared among the trees.

Rosie and Cleo went up to the acorn house and peeped through the window. Inside, a mother squirrel was playing with two babies, rolling a ball back and forth to them.

"That's so cute!" Rosie whispered. "They're having so much fun."

They peeked into the next cozy acorn house and spied two chipmunks drinking tea in front of the fire.

Rosie was really thirsty after digging her tunnel and running the race with Cleo. She was going to ask someone to get her a drink when she suddenly remembered that she wasn't at the palace—there weren't any servants around to help her!

Just then, the squirrel with the tufty ears scurried back.

"I can't go back home. Mom will be so mad!" he chattered, standing by the door of his acorn house.

His tail twitched and he bounded away again, scrabbling among the tree roots.

"Where, oh, where are they?" he muttered. "I have to find them!"

Rosie trotted over. "Did you lose something? My name's Rosie, by the way. And this is Cleo."

"I'm Charlie," the squirrel said. He

looked very worried. "I'm in BIG trouble. I found some hazelnuts, yesterday, the tastiest ones ever. I buried them to keep them safe, and now I can't remember where! It's really important that I find them, because they're a gift for someone really important. I'm such a silly squirrel!"

"You're not silly! Everybody loses things, especially me. My mom gets annoyed, too, especially when I lose my best ti—" Rosie was just about to say "tiara" but then she remembered that she was in the forest, where nobody knew she was a princess and nobody wore a tiara.

"Your best what?" Cleo asked.

"Oh, just my . . . er . . . my tin of dog biscuits."

"That's a big thing to lose."

"Well . . . I'm like Charlie. I put my, er, tin somewhere safe and then I forget where it is." Rosie wagged her tail, hoping her friend couldn't tell how uncomfortable she felt, telling a lie.

But Cleo didn't notice anything was wrong. "Come on," said the kitten. "Let's help Charlie find his nuts!"

Cleo padded away and began hunting among the ferns by the path, pushing the leaves aside with her paws.

Rosie was best at finding things with her

nose, so she sniffed around the tree roots. All she could smell was the little flowers that grew there.

Charlie was darting from tree to tree giddily. He was making Rosie feel quite dizzy with all his rushing around.

"I buried them in a hole," he jabbered. "A great big hole. But *where*?"

Rosie was feeling tired now from all her searching. She sat down by a tree trunk to rest. It wasn't very comfy. The bark was wrinkly and hard, and underneath her tail she felt something odd. Was it . . . a hole?

Rosie jumped up to investigate, sticking her nose inside the hole. *Sniff! Sniff!* Aha!

She could smell something nutty. "I found them!" she barked.

Charlie raced over, digging wildly with his front paws to get the nuts out. Earth flew everywhere as he dug.

Soon Rosie's fur was covered with even more dirt. She didn't mind, though, because Charlie looked so relieved as he stuffed hazelnuts into his cheeks.

"Thunk-oo! Thunk-oo sho mush!" he mumbled.

"You're welcome," Rosie yapped.

"Charlie?" his mother called. "Where are those nuts? We need to start getting ready!"

"Coming!" he shouted. Then the little

squirrel scampered off home, his cheeks bulging with his precious hazelnuts.

Cleo said something, but Rosie couldn't hear her. She shook her head, and bits of dirt fell out of her ears.

"That's better!" said Rosie. "What were you saying?"

"That we need to get you cleaned up!" Cleo said, gently combing Rosie's curly fur with her paws until all the soil was gone.

"Charlie's mother will be pleased about the nuts," Cleo meowed. "What's your mom like, Rosie?"

"Umm . . ." What should Rosie say? She couldn't give too much away, or Cleo might guess who she really was. "Well, she has curly fur . . ."

"Just like you!" Cleo purred.

"Not really," Rosie said, shaking her head. "My mom always looks very elegant. And she can be really strict!"

They started trotting down the path together. "My mom can be strict sometimes, too," said Cleo sympathetically.

"Well, Her Maj—"

Rosie froze. Oops! Did Cleo hear that?

Cleo looked puzzled. "Her what?"

Rosie thought fast. "Her, um, *major* thing is manners. She likes me to be really well behaved, which I find hard sometimes."

Rosie knew she needed to change the subject—and fast! It was just so easy to talk to Cleo. If she wasn't careful, her new friend would soon figure out who Rosie really was!

Up ahead, Rosie saw a bright flash of sunlight shining on water. "Look, Cleo!" she yapped. "There's a stream up ahead. It runs right across the path."

"Noooo!" Cleo yowled.

"What's wrong?" Rosie asked, puzzled. She'd distracted Cleo from talking about her mom, but she hadn't meant to upset her!

Cleo covered her eyes with her paws.

"I'm scared of water! I'll never be able to get across!"

Rosie's tail drooped. If Cleo wouldn't

cross the stream, they'd never be able to have all the exciting adventures that were waiting for them on the other side of the forest.

She HAD to persuade Cleo to cross the stream!

Chapter 5

Bridges and Blackberries

Rosie ran ahead and leaped into the stream. The water was rushing merrily along. It felt cool and fresh. She lapped some up with her tongue. It tasted wonderfully refreshing, too!

"Come on, Cleo! It's much better than a bubble bath!"

Cleo stayed on the path. The tip of her tail flicked back and forth nervously.

"I never take baths," she meowed.

"How do you say clean then?" Rosie asked.

"I wash myself like this, of course." Cleo licked her gray paw and delicately rubbed her face with it. "That's the proper kitten way."

"Really? That's fantastic!" Rosie wagged her tail, and water splashed everywhere. "I'm a puppy, so I can't do that. I have to take a bath at least twice a week!"

"Eeek!" Cleo jumped back from the splashes. "I don't even like to get water on my paws."

Rosie looked down. The rushing stream

came up to her stomach. There was no way that Cleo could cross it without getting soaked.

Rosie scrambled up the muddy bank and sat down to think. Then she jumped to her feet, her tail wagging. "I've got it!"

Not far from the bank, a big branch had fallen from one of the trees. Rosie dragged it toward the stream. It was hard work, pulling it along with her teeth.

"Grrrr! I wish Rollo and Rocky were here to help me!" she growled.

"Rocky and who?"

"Oh, nothing!" Rosie muttered. She had to stop saying things about the palace without thinking!

She tugged and dragged and huffed and puffed, and soon the branch was at the edge of the stream. There was just one last thing to do.

Rosie took hold of the branch and jumped into the stream again. She paddled to the other side, pulling the end of the branch with her. Then she rested it on the opposite bank.

"Wow, Rosie!" Cleo clapped her paws. "You made a bridge!"

"Yup, that's right!" Rosie scrambled up the muddy bank. "Come on, Cleo! You can cross over and stay dry now."

"Only if you stop wagging your tail," Cleo said, giggling. "Otherwise I'll get just as wet as if I had swam!"

Rosie kept her tail still, and watched the gray kitten as she trotted daintily over the branch. Not one drop of water touched her paws.

"Thank you!" Cleo meowed. Then she looked at her friend. "Oh, Rosie! You look like a big lump of mud with two eyes peeking out! Why don't you jump into the stream again to get clean. But this time, use the bridge to get out so you don't get muddy again."

Rosie did what her friend suggested. She washed the mud off in the water, and then pulled herself onto the bridge she'd made. Balancing carefully, Rosie crossed to the other side. She was soaking wet, and had lost all her daisy chains, but at least she was clean.

"Hey, Cleo, what's that sound?" Rosie asked. "Can you hear it, too?"

"Twee twee twooo! Twee tweety twoo!" A sweet voice was singing, high up in the trees.

Cleo and Rosie ran in the direction the music was coming from.

"It must be a bird." Cleo peered up into the green leaves.

It wasn't just one bird—there were lots of birds singing. Rosie's tail wagged with excitement.

"Look at the adorable little houses, Cleo! They must be where the birds live."

The birdhouses were painted all the colors of the rainbow. Just above Rosie's head there was a blue one with a bright yellow roof. A little higher up, there was a green house with an orange roof, and above that was a red one with a purple door and a pink chimney.

"Twitter Town!" Cleo read, from a sign that was fixed to a branch.

"That's the perfect name for this place," Rosie said happily, listening to the cheerful singing.

Then the two friends heard a funny little

noise coming from the long grass beneath the trees.

"Cheep, cheep!" It was a tiny baby bird, waving its stumpy wings.

"Oh dear. Your feathers haven't begun to grow yet," Cleo meowed. "I bet you can't fly, can you?"

The baby bird shook its head. "I want my mama!"

"Don't worry, we'll look after you. Which house is yours?" Rosie asked.

The little bird pointed a wing toward the blue house.

Rosie nudged the baby bird with her nose to help it climb onto her paw, and then she stood up on her hind legs to reach the blue birdhouse. "Hello?" she called. "Is anyone home?"

A bright black eye looked out of the door hole. It was the mother bird.

"There you are, Melody!" she chirped. "I was so worried! Come inside and cuddle up with your brothers and sisters. You'll have to wait a few more days before you try and learn how to fly!"

The baby bird waved good-bye to Rosie, then hopped through the hole and disappeared.

"Thank you so much!" the mother bird trilled. "I have so many babies in here it's hard to keep my eye on all of them!"

Then the father bird arrived. His beak was full of seeds, so he couldn't sing or speak, but he nodded his thanks to the two friends, and then he went inside.

"They're having their dinner," Rosie said, trying to remember the last time she'd had anything to eat.

GRRR! Rosie's stomach gave a loud rumble.

Cleo jumped in fright. "Why are you growling at me, Rosie?"

"I'm not. It's my stomach," Rosie explained. "I can't help it. I'm starving!"

GRRR! went Rosie's stomach again.

"We'd better find something to eat, then!"

Cleo meowed, and she trotted back to the path. Rosie followed her.

They soon came to some sort of village. Rosie could see fences everywhere, marking out neat gardens with flowers and vegetables growing in them. But where were the houses?

Then a small golden hamster popped up from a hole in the ground.

"Welcome to Hamster Hamlet!" she chattered. "I'm Elsie. This is my burrow. Who are you?"

Cleo and Rosie introduced themselves.

Elsie rubbed her little pink hands together. "I was just leaving to pick some blackberries. Do you want to come along?"

Rosie and Cleo nodded eagerly. Rosie's stomach rumbled in anticipation.

Elsie scurried off and they followed her to a big blackberry patch.

"The juiciest ones are always at the top of the bush," said Elsie. "You'll be able to reach them because you're taller than me."

The hamster laid out some leaves to hold the fruit, and the three of them started to pick the sweet dark purple berries.

"Yum!" Rosie sighed as she ate her tenth blackberry. "Pick one, eat one. I had no idea blackberries were so delicious!"

There was a plump blackberry right at the top of the bush, and Rosie jumped up to catch it in her paws. She missed, and down she fell through the bushes. Ouch! Now there were prickles all over her fur.

Rosie tried again. This time she caught the blackberry, but she held on to it much too tightly. *Splat!* Purple blackberry juice squirted all over her fur.

"Elsiiieee!" someone was calling from the burrow. "It's time to get ready!"

"That's my mom," Elsie squeaked. "I've got to go. Thanks so much for your help—we've got a ton of blackberries to take to the party now."

She scuttled away, pulling the leaves loaded with berries behind her.

Party?! Rosie sat down and hung her

head. She had a funny feeling in her stomach, and it wasn't from eating too many blackberries.

Any minute now, the garden party at Pawstone Palace would be starting. Everybody would be looking for her. She was going to be in very big trouble!

Chapter 6

Lost in the Woods

"Eeew, Rosie! You look like a hairy purple monster . . ." Cleo meowed.

Rosie lay down and burrowed her nose into her paws. Did she really look like a monster? Even if she made it to the party in time, nobody would recognize her, all sticky and purple!

"Never mind, I'll get you fixed up. I'm getting used to it now!" Cleo got to work picking the prickles out of Rosie's fur. Then she wet her paw and used the kitten method to wash away the squishy blackberry bits.

"There you go!" she purred as she licked the last drop of juice from her paw. "What's wrong, Rosie? You're all clean again. Don't look so sad! I know, why don't I make us some more daisy chains?"

"Thanks, Cleo. A daisy chain would be lovely. But it won't help. The thing is, I've to got to get home, as fast as I can. We're having a party."

"A party! Oooh! That sounds fun!" Cleo purred.

Rosie put her paws over her eyes. "But

I'm going to be late, Cleo, and Priscilla will be FURIOUS with me."

"Who's Priscilla?" Cleo asked. "Is she your mom?"

"No . . . well . . ." Rosie began.

But before she could think how to explain Priscilla, Elsie the hamster came scampering back with two walnut shell cups.

"I thought you two might be thirsty," she squeaked. "So we made you some blackberry juice."

"Mmmm, thank you!" Cleo purred. "Just what we needed!"

The two friends lapped up the delicious drink.

"Where are you going now?" Elsie asked.

"I'd love to stay in the forest and have more adventures," Rosie said. "But I've got to go back home. Except . . ."

Rosie looked around. How had she and Cleo gotten here? How were they going to find their way back? Rosie's tail drooped.

"I think we're lost . . ." she whimpered.

"Where do you live?" Elsie asked. "What's your house like? Is it a burrow, like mine?"

"Oh no. My house is huge . . ." Rosie began. "It reaches way up to the sky, and it's got lots of rooms."

"Wow!" Elsie squeaked.

"It sounds amazing. I'd love to see it!" Cleo meowed.

Rosie had the funny feeling in her tummy again. If Cleo ever came to Pawstone Palace, she would know that Rosie was a princess. Would she still want to be Rosie's friend? And what would Priscilla say?

Rosie was pretty sure that princesses weren't supposed to run around playing in the forest and making friends with kittens. Priscilla and Queen Fifi would be really annoyed with her.

Rosie hated the thought of saying good-bye to Cleo. Her tail drooped right down to the ground. Maybe it would be better to stay lost in the forest, and never find her way back home.

But Cleo was thinking. "Wait a minute," she meowed. "Remember where we met, Rosie? I bet you could find your way home from there."

Rosie nodded.

"Elsie, do you know those very tall pine trees at the edge of the forest?" Cleo asked. "Can you tell us how to get there?"

"Sorry," Elsie squeaked. "I've never been very far from my burrow. The only place I've ever visited is Twitter Town. I went with my family to hear the singing."

"That's where we came from! So it must be on the way home," Cleo meowed.

Elsie pointed out a big beech tree. "Turn left just there, and keep going straight until you see the birdhouses," she told the two friends. "Follow your ears and you'll soon reach Twitter Town. Good luck!"

"What would I do without you, Cleo?" Rosie yapped as they set off. "You're the smartest and most helpful kitten ever." She felt very sad to think that soon she would have to say good-bye to her new friend.

As the two of them arrived in Twitter Town, the mother bird darted out from the blue house.

"Hello again, girls! Little Melody is so happy to be back with her brothers and sisters!" she sang. "If there's ever anything I can do for you, just let me know."

"Actually, there is," Cleo purred. "We're lost. Do you know how to get to Oak Tree Hollow?"

The mother bird twirled in the air and flicked her wing to show them the way. "Keep going straight and you'll come to a stream. Cross the water, and you'll soon find the path to Oak Tree Hollow."

The two friends hurried through the

trees. In no time at all, they found them-selves back at the stream.

"Phew! I'm glad our bridge is still here," Cleo said as she trotted over the branch.

"I should use it, too," Rosie said. "It's quicker."

"You'll stay cleaner, too!"

When they were both safely across, they followed the path to Oak Tree Hollow.

"Hello!" Charlie the squirrel peeked out from his acorn home. "What are you two up to?"

"We're in a rush," Cleo explained. "Do you know the really tall pine trees at the edge of the woods? We're trying to get back there."

Charlie bounced across the path and started climbing a tall oak tree. "No, but I can soon spot them for you."

He scrambled up the trunk to the very top and held his paw above his eyes to help him see. "There they are!" he cried, pointing with his paw. "Great big pine trees. And I can see lots of daisies growing nearby."

"That's the place! Thanks, Charlie," Cleo meowed. "You're a hero."

"No problem. See you again sometime, I hope!" Charlie bounded down the trunk again as Rosie and Cleo raced along the path toward the pine trees.

But when they got there, Rosie couldn't find her tunnel. She started to panic.

"Where can it be?" she whimpered. "These are the pine trees where we met, but I can't find the tunnel I came through to get here. And I'm running out of time!"

"Don't worry," Cleo meowed. "Let's look around and see if you spot anything that looks familiar."

Rosie gazed around. This was hopeless! If she couldn't find her tunnel, she'd miss the whole party. And what did that mean? She'd be in even more trouble!

"Oh, look!" Cleo cried. "There's a pretty pink ribbon in that daisy patch."

"That's mine," said Rosie, relieved. "It's one of my pink bows! I took it off when I climbed out of the tunnel. That means the tunnel can't be far away."

"Don't worry. You'll find it soon, Rosie. I know you will," Cleo purred.

Rosie sniffed her way through the ferns until she found a pile of earth. It was the entrance to the tunnel! She turned back to Cleo and her heart sank. It was time to say good-bye.

"I've got to go now," she said reluctantly. Her eyes felt very hot, and she knew she was going to cry.

"Are you okay, Rosie?" Cleo came over and stroked her fur gently. "Do you want me to come with you?"

Rosie looked at the gray kitten. She

thought of all the fun they'd had today, and of all the times that Cleo had helped her. She really didn't want to say good-bye to her new friend. She wasn't sure what would happen when Cleo found out who she really was, but she'd just have to take that chance.

"Yes, please!" she barked. "Follow me!"

The two friends wriggled through the damp tunnel, and then—*POP!*—Rosie scrambled out onto the lush, green grass of the royal gardens. *POP!* Cleo climbed out after her.

They raced up the grassy slope together, and there, on the other side of the lawn, stood Pawstone Palace. Paw-print flags flew from every tower and in the distance was a tent and tables set out with platters of party foods.

"Oooh!" Cleo's blue eyes were like saucers. "Rosie, that's Pawstone Palace!"

"Yes," Rosie said, looking down at her paws nervously.

"This is the king's garden," Cleo babbled. "We'd better run. If somebody catches us—"

"It'll be all right. No one will yell at you. I won't let them," Rosie said.

"But you're just a puppy."

"WOOF! WOOF!" The sound of barking came across the grass.

"Uh-oh! Someone's coming!" Cleo's gray fur had gone spiky with fear.

Rollo and Rocky came racing across the lawn. The puppy princes were wearing emerald crowns and their best jeweled collars.

"Where have you been?" Rollo demanded.

"The party's about to start," Rocky announced.

"Let's run for it!" squealed Cleo.

Rosie put her paw around Cleo and held her friend tightly.

"It's okay. I can explain . . ." she began.

But then Rollo said, "Look what we found, hidden under a leaf! It's your tiara, Rosie! But we couldn't find YOU! Mom's going crazy."

He placed the diamond crown on Rosie's head.

Cleo stared at her friend in astonishment. Her big blue eyes looked wider than ever. "Oh my gosh!" she gasped. "You're . . . you're . . . PRINCESS Rosie?!"

Chapter 7

Rosie's Return

"I am." Rosie nodded sheepishly. "I'm sorry I didn't tell you."

"Your Royal Highness." Cleo bowed low. "I'm so honored to—"

"No, no!" Rosie shook her head so hard her tiara nearly flew off. "Stop! I'm just Rosie—your friend!"

DOO-DI-DOO-DI-DOOO! They heard the sound of a trumpet coming from the palace.

"The party's about to start," Rocky yapped. "But, Rosie, what HAVE you been doing? Rolling in the mud all day? It's going to take about a million baths to get you clean!"

Rosie went to the fountain and looked at her reflection in the pool. Her fur was tangled, her sparkly tiara was lopsided, and there wasn't a single pink ribbon tied in her curls.

Then a voice called, "Princess Rosie? Come out, wherever you are! This is no time for games!"

Rosie's lady-in-waiting was searching the rose bushes. Theodore the butler was helping, his short tortoise legs working hard to keep up with her hops.

"Run, Rosie!" growled Rocky. "Hurry— or you and your friend will be in big trouble. We'll take care of Priscilla and Theodore!"

"Follow me, Cleo!" Rosie hid behind some bushes. She and Cleo crawled along on their stomachs until they were hidden by the leaves. Cleo looked very confused.

"Rosie," she whispered. "Was that Priscilla we just saw? I don't understand. How can your mom be a bunny rabbit?"

"Shh!" Rosie whispered. "I'll explain later."

They peered through the leaves and saw

Rocky twitching his black nose, sniffing the air loudly. "I smell something funny," Rocky said. "I think it might be Pretty Pooch perfume."

"Really?" said Priscilla, her long ears pricking up. "Princess Rosie wears Pretty Pooch perfume!"

"I think it's coming from over there! Come on, Priscilla!" Rocky led the lady-in-waiting over to the farthest corner of the garden.

Rollo was left to distract Theodore. "Look, isn't that a pink ribbon?" He pointed with his paw in the opposite direction from where Rosie and Cleo were hiding.

"It might be. On the other hand, it's

probably just a pink rose, Your Highness," the old tortoise grumbled, blinking his shortsighted eyes.

"No, I'm pretty sure it's one of Rosie's ribbons!" Rollo yapped. "We'd better check it out! I'll race you, Theodore!"

He galloped off across the grass, with the butler crawling slowly after him.

Rosie and Cleo stayed hidden behind the leaves.

"Rosie, I thought your mom was named Priscilla."

"I didn't say that, not exactly," Rosie said. "I just didn't explain everything clearly. Priscilla's my lady-in-waiting."

"So who IS your mom?"

"Queen Fifi."

Cleo shook herself. "The queen, of course! Wow, Rosie! I still can't believe it. I'm friends with a real princess!"

Rosie's stomach felt very tight. "Listen, Cleo," she said anxiously. "Will you promise me something?"

"Of course, Your Highness!"

"I'd rather be just Rosie to you. Underneath my tiara I'm just a normal puppy. Please don't treat me any differently, now that you know who I am."

Cleo looked at her for a moment and then she said, "Rosie, we'll *always* be friends. Just like we were in the forest. I promise."

DOO-DI-DOO-DI-DOOO! tootled the trumpet.

"Oh noooo!" Rosie whimpered. "The guests are arriving. I should be there to greet them. But I can't go the party looking like this . . ."

She looked in dismay at her muddy paws, and felt her tiara sliding down onto her nose. "How do you stay so tidy, Cleo?"

"Because I'm a kitten," Cleo meowed. "We like to stay clean. But don't worry, I have a plan. Quick, Rosie! Get in the fountain—now!"

"Okay!" Rosie ran across the lawn and jumped into the fountain. She splashed around under the jets of water, getting clean. Taking a shower in the fountain was a lot more fun than taking a bath!

When all the mud was washed away, she jumped out again. "I'm clean, but now I'm soaking wet!"

But clever Cleo had a plan. "Roll in those flowers," she said, pointing to a patch of clover. "They'll get you dry in a flash."

Rosie rolled in the fluffy pink-and-white clover and then she shook herself off. "That's better," she barked.

"Now let's get you groomed!" Cleo combed Rosie's curls with her paws and fluffed them up. Then she reached for the pink ribbon she'd found near the tunnel.

"Yuck! I hate having bows tied in my fur," Rosie whined.

Cleo looked thoughtful. "Okay, let's try this." She smoothed out the ribbon and gently tied it in a pretty bow around Rosie's neck.

Rosie shook herself. "That feels nice. Really comfy."

"What's next?" Cleo asked.

"Normally I get sprayed with Pretty Pooch perfume. Priscilla says it smells nice, but I think it stinks!"

"You don't need perfume to smell nice," Cleo said. "What are your favorite flowers in the garden?"

Rosie trotted over to a big bush, which was covered in white roses. "I like these because they haven't got any thorns, *and* they smell amazing."

Cleo picked some of the roses and tucked them around the pink ribbon so they made a beautiful garland. Then she wove more roses into her friend's tiara.

"Mmmm," she purred. "You look fantastic

and you smell gorgeous. Princess Rosie, I mean, Rosie—you're ready for party time!"

"Thank you!" Rosie yipped. But then she heard a very loud "HUFF!"

"Uh-oh!" Rosie whimpered. "Priscilla's back!"

Chapter 8

Party Time!

"I found you at last, Princess Rosie!" called the lady-in-waiting. "Where have you been hiding? What have you done with all your bows?" She turned to glare at Cleo. "And who is this?"

Cleo's ears were flat against her head and her tail stuck straight up in the air. She looked terrified.

"Cleo," Rosie whispered. "Whatever you do, don't run!"

Rosie took a deep breath. "This is my friend Cleo!" she announced to Priscilla.

"*Friend*, Princess Rosie?" Priscilla was so furious she could hardly speak. "Puppy princesses don't have *kitten friends!!!*"

"This one does!" Rosie said defiantly.

"Princesses don't have time for friends," Priscilla said.

Rosie took another deep breath. Priscilla had so many rules about what a princess should and shouldn't do with her time. Suddenly, Rosie thought of two new rules of her own! ONE: A princess must ALWAYS be brave. TWO: A princess must NEVER let her friends down!

"Cleo is my best friend. We have fun together. We help each other. And I love having a friend to play with!" Rosie barked as loud as she could.

Priscilla was huffing so much Rosie thought she might explode any minute. Theodore the butler came creeping over.

"Be quiet, all of you!" he called in his creaky old voice. "Their Majesties are approaching!"

"Oh no! I should probably go," Cleo said nervously.

"Don't leave me, please!" Rosie

whimpered. "The party won't be any fun without you."

Queen Fifi came trotting gracefully across the lawn. Her head was held high, and she was wearing a diamond and ruby crown to match her red-painted nails.

King Charles waddled along behind the queen. He was wearing a heavy gold crown, studded with jewels. "Well, bless my whiskers!" he barked. "Rosie, we thought we'd lost you!"

"The princess has been extremely troublesome!" Priscilla began. "She ran away . . . huff, huff! She's lost all her beautiful pink ribbons . . . huff, huff, huff . . .

And she's found herself a most unsuitable *FRIEND!*"

"Hush, Priscilla!" Queen Fifi raised one of her elegant paws. "A lady-in-waiting should ALWAYS be calm. She should NEVER babble. I can see that Princess Rosie still has one of her ribbons. And she's wearing some beautiful roses. Rosie, perhaps you can explain what has been going on?"

"Yes, of course, Mom—I mean, Your Majesty," Rosie said. "I was playing in the gardens and I got messy. I didn't want Priscilla to make me take another bath, so I thought of a way to hide . . ."

Rosie was about to explain about King Charles digging a tunnel when he was a puppy, but she decided not to tell in case Hamish got into trouble. "I burrowed through the earth and then I came out on the other side of the wall."

"That reminds me of the kind of thing I used to do when I was a pup!" King Charles said approvingly.

"I knew it was bad to leave without telling anyone," Rosie continued. "But I was so curious to see what Petrovia was like outside of the palace. Everything was so beautiful. But best of all, we made so many new friends. Squirrels and birds and hamsters and . . ."

"We?" Queen Fifi said.

Rosie could feel Cleo trembling as she stood beside her. Rosie was scared, too. But then she remembered her new rule. A princess must ALWAYS be brave!

"Mom, Dad, this is Cleo. I met her in the forest. She's my best friend."

"I-I'm very sorry, Your Majesty," Cleo stammered. "I d-didn't k-know Rosie was a p-princess."

Queen Fifi looked down her nose at Cleo. "Is that so?" she said in her most regal voice. Cleo shook even more.

Then Queen Fifi smiled, showing her gleaming white teeth. "Cleo, you have nothing to apologize for. I looked out of my bedroom window while I was getting ready for the party and I saw you with my daughter. I watched you help her get clean and dry. I saw how you tied her ribbon in a perfect bow, and decorated it with the loveliest roses."

Now the queen turned to look at Rosie. "In fact, I have never seen the princess look so happy or well put together. Cleo, you are kind, clever, and loyal. I think you would be a perfect lady-in-waiting for my daughter. What do you say?"

Rosie looked at her friend. Cleo was too surprised to say anything at all.

Priscilla looked as though she'd like to say *lots* of things, but all that came out was: "HUFF-HUFF!"

King Charles stepped forward and patted Priscilla reassuringly. "Don't worry,

Priscilla. We would like to offer you a pro-motion. How would you like to be our chief housekeeper, in charge of keeping the palace in tip-top shape?"

"CHIEF HOUSEKEEPER? Oh yes!" Priscilla hopped for joy. "Will I get a new uniform, Your Majesty?"

"Absolutely!" King Charles barked. "Why don't you go to the palace tailor right away and get measured."

Priscilla bounced off toward the palace, muttering to herself excitedly. "First, I'll polish the silver water bowls! Next, I'll dust all the royal portraits . . ."

King Charles turned to Cleo. "Well, my

dear? What's your answer? Would you like to be Rosie's lady-in-waiting?"

"Oh yes!" Cleo gasped. "Of course I would! I need to ask my mom first, but I'm sure she'll be really proud. It's the most fantastic thing that's ever happened to me!"

Rosie wanted to howl for joy and run around the royal gardens wagging her tail, but she knew she'd better sit still and behave like a proper puppy princess for a little bit longer.

Queen Fifi stood up. "Come along, everyone. Our guests are here. We have work to do. Rosie, your special duty today will be to welcome our guests. Cleo, you will receive the presents and keep them safe."

"Presents, Your Majesty?"

"Our guests always bring gifts to the palace," Queen Fifi explained as they headed toward the garden gates.

A long line of animals from all over Petrovia was waiting at the gates. "Welcome, everybody!" King Charles barked as two guinea pig soldiers opened the gates.

Queen Fifi stood next to her husband. "How nice to see you. We hope you will enjoy yourselves," she said.

Rosie was next in line. "Thank you so much for coming," she said.

"This way for the food!" Prince Rollo and Prince Rocky barked together. "There's plenty for everyone!"

The guests kept on arriving. A family of squirrels was next in line.

Cleo nudged Rosie. "Look—isn't that Charlie?"

Their squirrel friend was carrying a big basket of hazelnuts.

"Oh my!" Charlie said, staring at Rosie. "Princess Rosie helped me find my lost nuts! Here, Your Highness. The hazelnuts are a special present for you!"

"Thank you, Charlie," Rosie said as Cleo took the basket from him. "Have fun at the party—my brothers will show you around!"

King Charles was listening to all this

with his head cocked to one side. He looked very thoughtful.

Then, with a flutter of wings, the mother and father bird Rosie had met earlier in the day appeared.

"Tweet, tweet! We can't stay long," the father bird said. "But we'd like to sing a special song for the royal family."

They chirped the sweetest tune Rosie had ever heard. When the birds had finished singing, everyone clapped their paws.

"Now we must dash!" the mother bird said. "Our babies are waiting at home! Melody will be thrilled to know it was Princess Rosie who saved her today!"

"What are they talking about?" King Charles asked Cleo.

"Rosie saved a baby bird who fell out of her house," Cleo explained.

Next, Elsie and her family arrived. "Look, Mom and Dad!" squeaked the little hamster. "It's Rosie and Cleo! They helped me pick these blackberries!"

"Here, Princess Rosie," said Elsie's dad. "The blackberries are a gift for you and your family."

"Thank you," Rosie said. She offered one to her father. "Try one, Dad—they're delicious!"

"Don't mind if I do," King Charles said, popping a few berries in his mouth.

The party went on for a long time. The grown-up guests chatted, ate the delicious food, and admired the flower beds.

The younger guests ate lots of yummy food, too, and played with the puppy princes in the royal gardens.

When the party was over and all the guests had gone home, Queen Fifi and King Charles came over to Rosie and Cleo.

"You were a perfectly polite puppy princess today, Rosie," said Queen Fifi. "Thank you. I can see that Cleo is a very good influence on you."

"I'm proud that you helped so many people today, Rosie," said King Charles. "I think you might be ready to take on more royal duties—especially now that you have a friend by your side." He smiled at Rosie and Cleo and then winked. "But for now, why don't you two go have some fun."

"Yay!" Rosie cried.

She and Cleo scampered off. They ran past Priscilla, who was hopping about in her new uniform, tidying up. She was saying to Theodore, "A chief housekeeper ALWAYS clears away the mess. She NEVER leaves even a crumb behind."

Rosie grinned at Cleo. "I think Priscilla has found the perfect job. Now she can boss Theodore around instead of me! And I've got the best lady-in-waiting I could ever wish for!"

"I'm so happy!" Cleo purred. "This is a dream come true! I'll never let you down, Rosie."

Rosie smiled. "Thanks, Cleo. I won't let you down, either. Actually, there's one thing you can do for me right now."

"Of course, Your Highness." Cleo jumped to attention. "What do you need?"

Rosie's eyes twinkled mischievously. "I need you to . . . CATCH ME!"

Rosie took off, racing across the green lawn.

"You might be a princess, but I'm still going to get you!" Cleo giggled and chased after her.

Rosie barked happily, her ears streaming

behind her as she bounded across the grass. Having a best friend was worth more than being a princess or having a palace full of jewels. As she played tag with Cleo in the late afternoon sunshine, Rosie knew she was the luckiest puppy in all of Petrovia!

Read on for more Puppy Princess fun!

Puppy Princess #2
Super Sweet Dreams

"Oh, hello, girls," the queen said. "I didn't expect to see you two in here."

"I was showing Cleo the royal jewels," Rosie said. It was true—sort of.

"I like the gold-and-ruby tiara, Your

Majesty," Cleo said shyly. "It matches your collar."

"I agree," Queen Fifi said, smiling. "Rosie, your lady-in-waiting has excellent taste. This is one of my favorites. It was a birthday present from the king."

"Wow!" Cleo sighed. "What a beautiful birthday gift!"

Rosie suddenly realized something. She didn't know her best friend's birthday. "Cleo, when's your birthday? Mine's in July."

"Actually," Cleo said. "It's coming up soon—it's in two days."

Rosie gulped. She only had two days to think of a special birthday gift for Cleo. There was no time to lose!